"THE READING GROUP"

&

"A BRIGHT WOMAN"

L TAYLOR

ISBN   9798393314569

Story 1

THE READING GROUP

Mo finished tidying the last cushion on her reproduction Regency sofa and took one last sweep with her duster at the shiny mahogany, tripod table placed between the three Regency-style comfy chairs, with arms and cabriole legs. She stood back from the room and took one final check at the whole room. It was just as she wanted and had slowly managed to create, saving money here and there to buy each piece of furniture. The reproduction Secretaire bookcase, the most expensive piece of furniture in the room, was so like one featured in a Jane Austen film. The pale wallpaper added further light to this sunny room. On the fireplace wall, she had one terribly expensive mock paper with birds and trees. Over £90 a roll it had cost but well worth it, despite her husband David's horror at such an expense and his anxiety when hanging it. Though seldom necessary to switch them on at this time of year with the natural light that penetrated this room, the chandelier light fitting, wall lights and the lamps all matched and set the scene beautifully. And a set scene it was, for the

Reading Group of six would soon be seated here and ready to have some fun reading out their own works or from a favourite novel and every month reading together a chosen play from the local library. Thank goodness that despite these hard financial times- which seemed a regular 'guest' over the last few decades- the local library had been given some central government funding to refurnish and keep it open!

The group had been coming now for several months and no one ever seemed to feel overawed by the room. At first sight, it had been met with appreciative gasps of "wow" and "my word"' plus broad smiles. Even now, before taking their seats the ladies would mutter, "Such a *lovely* room, Mo!' Having noted how popular they were in stately homes, she had further added black and white photographs of her siblings at various ages, within costly silver frames. Two were no longer alive and the three others were somewhat detached but they remained important to her, especially as she and David had not been blessed with children. David was orphaned and knew nothing of his family background.

Mike was the first of the group to arrive. She now recognised the sound of his car as it crunched over the gravel. He would have to park in front of their garage doors as, of late, this road was getting more crowded with parked cars due to the new estate being built where once stood a grammar school. People had to park somewhere but it was a shame they chose this road. Most were also retired people and Mo guessed they parked up as early as they could. He rang the bell and Mo tripped lightly along her hallway to greet him. One got used to his twitching tic over time, although at first, newcomers would look away politely only to discover that the rabbit-like nose twitch was not a one-off or occasional habit but one he seemed unaware of doing and doing it frequently. If he was aware of doing it, surely he would try to suppress it? She did wonder why he did it, how long he had been doing it and whether to ask him about it. But so far, she did not feel enough of a friend to him to do so. In fact, would a friend dare ask such a question? It was a quandary and no one so far had taken the risk of offending Mike by asking him about it and what, if anything, had caused it. He was divorced and had three grown-up children. This personal information he had willingly offered at the first group meeting when Mo had encouraged everyone to say something about themselves for the others, if only to announce their name.

'Nice day again, Mo. I trust we have a full complement...' he said, as he stepped in beside her. His towering figure of at least six foot six meant he had to stoop down toward her thin, five-foot frame; somewhat resembling a walking stick, Mo always thought, trying not to smile too broadly at the similarity. But then Mike could hardly greet her by speaking over her short-cropped head! He peered into her wrinkled face and dared to wonder at her age before the first twitch told hold. She was wearing those ghastly, polyester beige trousers and a blouse and cardigan. But despite her rather jaded apparel, he liked her for her kindness and gentle manner. He had no truck with those modern, aggressive females which was why he seldom saw his only daughter and the only child still living in the U.K. His two 'Boys', as he still called them, had successful careers overseas which left him needing to socialise and join a group. He was still working on the first chapter of his memoirs but doubted if they would be of much interest to the group and so preferred reading plays which would be today's given task. Maybe he would never finish the book and if he ever succeeded in doing so, he would probably have to pay a publisher to print it.

Shazi arrived next. Shazi was short for Shazadi which she had soon informed the group meant 'beautiful one' and had been chosen by her beloved Papa. She was dressed as ever in a Bohemian style: a tasselled and colourful, woollen shawl over a knitted waistcoat, a thin undervest and a long thick cotton fabric skirt. Flat-laced shoes peeked out as she swished across the ground revealing the odd bit of dark stocking. She was tall but not quite as tall as Mike with short, almost crew-cut hair that lay flat to her small head and yet flattered her high cheekbones, long nose and sharp blue eyes. Mo had never seen her wear any kind of makeup or cover the wrinkles and odd mole but her face bore a natural, healthy glow. She was strictly vegetarian so Mo had to be careful not to offend her by offering shop-bought cake or biscuits.

Shazi bent down to offer her cheek, always so warm, and pressed it against Mo's in welcome. At first, Mo had considered this a rather familiar greeting but soon adapted to it and readily awaited and accepted it. Shazi was a kind, thoughtful soul and never meant offence. She whipped off her shawl as she took her seat beside Mike, her wooden beads swinging freely from her braless chest. Mo noticed that kind of thing but doubted if Mike or anyone else had done so. She prided herself in her observations and accuracy in recognising personalities. Like the others of the group,

Shazi merely glanced at Mike to avoid paying too much attention to his 'unfortunate habit' as she had, in his absence, once described his tic.

'And how are you keeping, Mike?' she enquired, sitting back against a satin cushion. Being so tall, she suffered with her back but found these seats comfortable enough for the two hours seated.

'Oh, not so bad, you know, Shazi. Off to Oz for a month soon.'

'To visit one of your sons, I suppose?'

'Yes. He wants some help with his tax

returns and sent me a return ticket! I expect

I can lose that for him in Expenses!'

Shazi laughed. It was a deep, manly laugh.

Having delved into it and found her

spectacles, she put her cloth bag down

beside her seat. She now fixed the chain

that hung from them around her neck,

placed the spectacles over her nose and

leaning forward took a copy of today's Play

from the coffee table where Mo had just

put a pile ready for reading.

'Oh, a comedy, I see. Who chose that, I forget whose turn it was…?' She flipped through the thin volume.

'It was Carl, dear. I've put a carafe of water there on the side and some glasses… should anyone wish to partake….' Mo explained and then heard the doorbell ring and hurried away to greet the next guest.

'I should have guessed as much…' Mike spoke softly but met with no response. He had often observed how big Shazi's hands were but had not yet had the time or occasion to ask Mo if she was really a woman or one of those "Trans" people. Of course, one had to be careful how one brought up such questions, especially when around the more modern and aggressive women of today. Women's Lib, as they called it, had a lot to answer for as he knew to his cost when his Ex had asked for a divorce.

Mo opened the door to Kathy. She frowned as usual despite Mo's smile of greeting and offering to shake her hand. Kathy's hand was plump yet cold and her handshake short and swift. She was not much taller than Mo but she carried a lot more weight. Mo had soon realised her love of food having noticed how she helped herself to

more than one biscuit or cake at a time. She

would secret them in her cupped hands,

look upward and around guiltily and Mo

would look away and busy herself as best

she could. It was comforting to see people

enjoy whatever she had to offer as a snack

so she didn't much mind, except for the

other members who were not so discreet

and would cast knowing looks at each other

on seeing Kathy's greed. Mo had observed

how fat some women now were and that

included the younger ones. She had read

about the problem many women had in

their relationship with food and felt

concerned, mixed with some intolerance at

such a lack of self-control. But then David

had often remarked how orderly and

sensible she was so she tried hard not to

judge either the overweight or indeed the

underweight too harshly. David's good

opinion of her had always, and would

always, mean so much to her.

'Carl's motorbike, I can hear it now...' Mo

exclaimed as Kathy took a seat on the

canary-coloured sofa. She plumped her fat

bottom down onto it squashing flat two of

the cushions and sighed heavily. No doubt

she would soon tell of her latest problem.

She opened the door and saw Carl's usual

big grin as he was standing beside the

newest member, Lauren.

'Come on in, do! We haven't started

without you.'

'I shouldn't think you could, old gal! 'Carl

laughed, his laughter sounding hiss-like as if

he wasn't so sure about letting it free. Mo

liked Carl. He was forty at least and yet had

retained a boyishness that charmed her

despite what the other members said of

him. People could be so intolerant at times.

Dressed in his usual short, padded jacket and worn denim jeans, he stepped inside and wiped his boots on the mat.

'Should I take 'em off, this time?' he asked, recalling how some mud had fallen onto her black and white tiled hallway on his last visit. Mo remembered the smell of his feet and shaking her head, laughed lightly, 'No, no, no need, Carl and welcome!' Sweeping up the odd bit of dry mud was surely better than such an odour. And of course, the weather had been drier so the chance of mud was less likely.

'Lauren, this is your second meeting! You might remember some names. How are you?' She enquired kindly, taking the younger woman's padded anorak from her and putting it up on a coat hook.

'I'm doing good, Mo, thanks.' She replied and gave that silly, girlish giggle. Mo had noticed that endless giggle last visit and put it down to nerves. Lauren had obviously not yet overcome them so she would work at making her feel more relaxed. Hopefully, the play that cheeky Carl had chosen and which she had already perused, would lighten the atmosphere and prove a winner.

Lauren was wearing a baggy, beige, jumper over a mini-skirt and the skirt was worn over thick, black, net stockings which, as Lauren walked in front towards the lounge, Mo noticed were showing odd holes. Mo wasn't sure if this was a new fashion or not. She had been horrified, as had David, at the sight of the fashion of young men letting their trousers or jeans hang so low below their waistlines that their underpants were left showing. Possibly Lauren had not noticed those holes. Should she discreetly mention it to her or would that offend? She decided to say nothing and hoped that the six pairs of eyes that had already arrived would refrain from focusing too long on them.

The play caused some laughter and went down well. It was about a bigamist whose daughter from one marriage met and fell for the only son of the other marriage and the problems this caused. Carl had to be prompted whenever his character was supposed to 'speak' but this was usual and the other players seemed to accept it. Only Kathy was heard to sigh once or twice with impatience. She hoped Carl had not taken heed of those heavy sighs, although she doubted if he would be that bothered if he had. But one could never be too sure of people. He was a laid-back, easy-going character. Lauren had giggled even more than on the earlier occasion, so Mo giggled with her, thinking it might help. The proof of this would be seen, or not, at the next meeting.

The one unsettling incident, during their hour-and-a-half play reading, was Mo noticing, as did Kathy, who had indicated so with the nod of her head toward Lauren's perpetual staring at Mike. This was her first time meeting him and she had begun to react most unexpectedly. She was seen twitching her face each time he twitched his nose! As far as the two ladies could gather, Mike had not noticed her doing this. Lauren's twitch was around her mouth. Had she had a twitch before? Could Mo have failed to notice it before? Could it be a new habit she had acquired, an odd reaction? Or was it a form of mockery? What was she to do or say and to whom?

Mo made coffee and tea as requested and Shazi came to help her as she would insist on doing. It was a kind gesture on her part and gave her the opportunity of updating Mo with her latest news regarding her only child, a troublesome daughter who had got mixed up with drugs, taken into hospital a few times and was now in a Mental Institution. According to Shazi, she was on the mend. Mo had talked to David about this daughter of 40 years of age and he had agreed that Shazi was being over-optimistic about such a change in the daughter. Both concluded that it was surely the only way

Shazi could cope: to have hope or to despair

and it was wise of her to choose the former.

It was at such times that Mo felt less sad

about not giving David a child, as children

could be so damaging.

 Tea and coffee were consumed quickly and

her homemade biscuits were popular and

soon grabbed into Kathy's chubby hands.

Karl and Lauren were the first to leave and

as the hostess, Mo naturally saw them to

the door. She looked intensely at Lauren.

'Is there something wrong?' Lauren asked,

then distracted, began to frantically search

for an umbrella in her copious, black

shoulder bag. 'God, I hate it when it rains!'

'You want a lift, gal?'

Lauren seemed to ignore Karl's offer.

'I couldn't borrow one, could I, Mo?' she

pleaded.

'Yes, of course dear, if you promise to

return it with the one you borrowed last

time.' Mo took in a deep controlling

breath.

'Oh, did I? Sorrwee!' She giggled, in tune

with the odd childish word she used on

embarrassing or awkward occasions.' Me,

velly forgetful at times.'

Mo could see no twitch at her mouth now.

She took a sunflower-patterned one out

from the umbrella stand but held it tightly

in her hand, intent on speaking her mind

before handing it over.

Karl, possibly sensing trouble, opened the

door, called out 'Cheers!' and just left the

two together in the hallway.

Mo could hear Shazi washing up the tea

things. She wished she would desist even

though the gesture was meant kindly. The

cups were never finished clean when Shazi

had 'helped out 'and the cake plates were

merely brushed free of crumbs.

Boldly, Mo asked the girl outright, 'Have

you got a tic, dear?'

Lauren looked aghast at the question. Mo's

heart beat faster in her chest. Oh, dear, had

she mishandled it already?

'Tic? Why, no, he's been done... he was

such a good boy too.'

Just at that critical moment, Mike called out

from the living room, 'Okay if I use your

phone, Mo. My mobile's flat!'

'Yes, of course... go ahead!' she quickly

replied. She turned her gaze back onto

Lauren whilst still clutching the umbrella

tightly.

'So, can I?' the girl asked, frowning. The rain

could be heard teeming down outside.

Lauren had just opened the door and held it

ajar when she hesitated. 'Was someone

itching then?' she asked giggling.

'It wasn't funny. He can't help it, Lauren.'

Mo stated, anger rising like indigestion after

a too hot curry.

'Sorry?'

Mo lowered her voice just in case Mike had

finished on the phone and might be on his

way to depart.

'Mike has an unfortunate … one, a nervous habit and I won't have people in the group acting so unfeeling, so cruelly!'

Lauren lowered the held umbrella. 'Oh, you mean the *other*…' she realised.

'Err, yes, exactly! And if yours is real, although I had not noticed before and I beg your pardon for bringing it up now… but if you suffer too, surely you might be more considerate…'

'I've lost you! I must go now… so sorry if I have somehow upset you. I really did enjoy the play…. My bus is due soon.'

Mo shook her head lightly. Was she going mad? Was this giggly girl being serious? Her patience was rapidly dribbling away like the rain dribbling down the window panes.

'Tic, tic, tic! You MUST know what I am talking about!' her voice grew louder and angry.

'I, I, I... need to get back. Buster will want a wee, you see and I don't want him doing it indoors. I'll get him checked out again then...'

Suddenly the sheer horror of her mistake hit Mo. Her throat felt dry, her stomach a bit queasy.

Lauren was almost out the door when Mike

appeared. He was known to tread softly.

Kathy had called it creepy.

'Let me give you a lift, Laura... err, Lauren, it

is Lauren isn't it!' he offered.

'Oh, thanks. I won't need this now then,

Mo.' She swiftly handed back the unopened

umbrella.

Mo looked at Mike. He was twitching again.

She then turned to look at Lauren who

merely seemed more confused than ever

and looked towards Mo and then back at

Mike. Mo took another deep breath. Lauren

did not twitch. Thank God! So was it a one-off reaction? She wished them both goodbye and watched them hurry down the path toward Mike's car. Lauren seemed to slam the door to her side as he pulled away.

Shazi was surprised to hear Mo laughing to herself as she joined her in the kitchen. 'What is it, is it something I said or did?' Mo continued to laugh. 'No, Shazi, it was nothing really... merely what he or she didn't do!'

'You've lost me, sweetie. I've done the washing up. Has Kathy gone yet? I've forgotten to give her back this book she loaned me. God, it was so miserable... as if I need to read something miserable. All about a Victorian Asylum, would you believe? Have you noticed how people these days, since the pandemic, are now so self-absorbed that they don't listen, they don't communicate properly....

'Oh yes, dear, I heartily agree!' Mo turned her back on Shazi, grinning now but managing to contain her laughter at her lack of "proper" communication.

Shazi and Kathy left together. Mo went to straighten the cushions and check her beloved, showpiece room.

A little later, as she was rewashing the china and cutlery in the kitchen, she heard David arrive home.

'High, my lovely!' he said, as he always did, and standing behind her bent and kissed the nape of her neck. 'How did the play reading go?'

Mo giggled girlishly. Was she catching mannerisms now, copying poor little Lauren? She must make the time to take her aside and explain at the next meeting.

As she had not yet replied, David

commented, 'A challenging one, was it?'

'Oh, yes, dear, you could say that! And who

knows what the next one will bring!'

Story 2

<u>A BRIGHT WOMAN</u>- a

<u>monologue/monodrama (in Alan</u>

<u>Bennett mode)</u>

Just like everyone else, I never liked

Mondays. Weekends were never long

enough, especially for someone like me,

living alone again with no one to help. I

worked hard at setting each marriage

straight. I didn't give up easily on

husband one, two, or three. Ironically,

for once all three readily agreed with me

to not prolong the marriage. Eventually,

I could see where I was going wrong. In

truth, they were all doomed to fail. I

attract the wrong sort; the kind of men

who don't want someone too attractive,

which I admit I never have been.

Someone who seemed easy, cosy, and a

good housekeeper. As soon as I made a

few minor demands, like sharing the

housework, and their learning to cook...

off they went with someone else.

Usually some tarty, younger girl. I

wasn't brought up to wear low-cut tops

and short skirts. The first two husbands

liked that about me. Probably they felt

less threatened. The first, Harry, said the

way I kept covered up gave me an air of

mystery, whatever that was supposed to

mean. He didn't repeat that comment

though. Our honeymoon put paid to

that. Total disaster! Now I'm no prude, I

know how the world works. But some

of the things he thought I should be

willing to do now I was his wife…

Where do they get their ideas from?

Porn, I guess.

As to Felix, my final effort...I've never been the sort to give up too easily... he was as cold as a frozen cucumber lying next to me. He preferred keeping company with his best mate. He never would give up seeing him and went off for weekend fishing trips with him. Fishing trips! Fishing at what I'd like to know. This young male friend took him in when I threw him out. I blame mothers, they will spoil boys much more than girls. I should know, my only sibling Thomas came to no good. He thought the world owed him a living.

Took after father. Well, he would,

wouldn't he? Even though father was

seldom home, the drunken pig!

Money sharing is the hardest thing for

men to do. Of course, my earning more

than all three of them, working in

Management at the bank, didn't help.

But even so, fair's fair and I expected a

share of their salaries. Marriage is a

contract, a combination of demand and

supply.

Harry started borrowing money. I followed him one day and despite having found betting tickets in his pockets and my telling him he should pay me some housekeeping before squandering the rest of his wages, he kept on betting. Wasting more and more of it but he was wasting more of mine! He had to go.

Number two now, Clive, we were together the longest- five years. Quiet as a mouse and boring but a no-goer. I realised too late, I would get nowhere with him! And everyone wants to buy not rent. These days renting is getting as big as a mortgage and its dead money. I worked in a bank, for goodness sake. I knew all about money handling.

Clive said he had friends in the pub and wanted to go and join them after working all week. I wasn't prepared to go with him, even if I had been asked, just to sit in that smelly, shabby old pub he called his regular. Being a good sort, I admit I did accompany him just once, but off he soon went, whisky in hand, talking to 'friends' he called them and leaving me to sit alone. No one approached me, fortunately.

One day, my suspicions aroused, I followed him to the pub. It was fun because I found this wig and outfit in a charity shop. I went in and he was nowhere to be seen. Then I heard that high-pitched laugh of his, seldom heard any more at home and I realised he was playing some card game held in the upstairs room. He must have won, because whilst I was having a quick half of lemon and lime at the bar, not wanting to raise suspicions or be recognised, I distinctly heard his voice call out 'drinks on me, guys!' And then, when I confronted him and told him I had found out about his secret card games, he raised a hand to me. That was it. End of story. I'd witnessed enough of that living with Father. So here I am, on a Monday lunchtime, kept waiting on her arrival, having just had two lightly boiled eggs. *Her* is Maggie Lawson and she lives opposite me. She has the top floor flat of the house and doesn't own a house as I do.

Her husband, of twenty years, would you believe- how she managed that is another of life's mysteries- works for the Gas Board, as a fitter. I twisted my ankle, you see, getting out of my Fiat. I'd had this accident with another driver ramming straight into the back of me. Driving too close of course although he denies it and says I wasn't looking in my mirror when I reversed to park up nearby. I can't say park up outside my drive because someone else always manages to take my space. Neighbour

Maggie offered to do some shopping for me because of my ankle. This arrangement has been going on now for a few weeks. I suppose I will have to remove the bandage and say my ankle is better but I don't want to upset her, she didn't have to volunteer to help me. The reason she did of course is that she's such a busybody. She claims, whispering it to me confidentially as if she was some kind of friend- that'll be the day!- that she was sweeping the path leading to the house she lives in and she saw me at the wheel and that I didn't look in my mirror when I reversed! However, I only had one mirror at the time, due to some rude local lads on bikes who tear down the avenue, wreaking revenge on all and sundry, including myself for heaven knows what reason. I am the politest person imaginable. I don't encourage confrontation. I'm sure those lads had the second mirror off. I didn't see them do it but then why do they always grin so cheekily, knowingly, whenever they see me out and about?

Here she comes. Wait for it... ''*Cooeee!*

It's only me!' I leave the latch up so that I

don't have to get up and go to the door.

What replacement goods has she chosen

this time, I wonder? Funny, when I

shopped for myself I always found the

brands I'm used to. And her

commenting how much cheaper it was,

each time she shows me the alternative,

niggles me. Is she asking for some kind

of praise and doing this on purpose?

I can hear the plod of her flat footsteps across the hall tiles and her heavy breathing. She should lose some of that body fat. I have probably been doing her some good on that score, letting her shop and carry. Yet last Monday, she had the audacity to comment that I had put on weight since my accident. Rubbish! If I took the trouble to weigh myself, which I can see no reason to do, I know I am the same weight I was as a girl. I might have a little temporary fluid retention due to my enforced lack of exercise, that's all. How could that silly creature understand? She isn't worth telling. Envy is the ugliest emotion. I was always a bright child, then brighter still as I grew into a young woman and thus my successful career was a forgone conclusion. I couldn't help it, could I? Nature gives what nature gives. Some would say nature is the fairest of all and gives deservedly.

Unfortunately, the chap who pranged my car wasn't happy to just exchange names and addresses, unlike the other two incidents when the drivers were more understanding. I fear it could go legal and add more points to my license. As if I need that extra worry, especially when not once was it my fault. So I need to keep Maggie sweet.

****

Thank goodness, she and her prattle

will soon be gone. Peace at last and next

Monday will be like all the other

Mondays but not quite as bad as these

last few. Not that I like visiting that

Supermarket. I worked there for a while

after the bank made me redundant.

Hated it, but I needed to finish the

mortgage payments and there were

absolutely no other vacancies locally or

within a decent mile radius. After some

weeks of failing to find me a worthy,

suitably paid situation, this incompetent

man at the Job Centre announced that he was going to be 'utterly frank' with me because he could tell I preferred frankness. He then went on to say that ex-bank employees in our town, of which of course there were many after said bank sent the jobs overseas, were not seen as viable prospects. I was outraged and he could see it. I asked what he meant and he smiled superciliously and replied that like ex-forces personnel, ex-bank employees were seen by local businesses as having a rigid mindset! I stormed out of there.

Libellous, surely! If I could only have

been bothered to take it up with

someone. I was sure it was ageism but

how to prove it?

As it happens, I saw a postcard in a local shop window for cashiers and so I applied and naturally I got the job at the Supermarket. Regrettably, some of the staff still recognise me from when I was employed there and probably recall that I was used to a managerial position. I soon found out how they knew. An ex-colleague's daughter worked there filling shelves and it had to be she who spread rumours that I was some kind of 'Tartar' to anyone under my supervision. Probably wanted a job as a cashier and to push me out. I didn't need to work there for long but that frostiness remains despite my now being a good, paying customer. That evil envy… need I repeat myself? Now she'll reorganise my kitchen cupboards, use the steps and warn me again that I mustn't try yet to mount them. I really will have to let her know I'm okay now.

I heard my cat, Pavlova coming through the cat flap. Bless her white socks, she must be hungry or it has started to rain again. As I approach the kitchen, not hopping so much with my walking stick, I hear Maggie, her voice sharp and unkind call at her, 'Shooo! Shooo!' She claims cats don't like her and start her asthma. Cats, I have found, have excellent judgment. I suppose I must oblige by moving her to the living room. She has her miniature, velvet chaise-longue in there, beside the fire.

'I can't thank you enough, Maggie but I feel I can manage now. By next Monday, I won't need this bothersome bandage and although my car is out of bounds, so to speak, I can easily take a taxi or a bus…'

'I wouldn't hear of it!' she smiles, revealing her nicotine-stained lower teeth. It seems more like a grimace.

'Now, now… you've known me long enough to realise how independent I am…' I begin.

She merely utters 'Ummm.' I do so hate

people who Umm and Aaah.

'Well, if you're sure…'

I see her to the door, but not before

handing her a brown, wages envelope

that doesn't clink as she clasps it tightly

in her palm. It holds a fair wad of paper

notes as a thank you and I trust enough

for her silence on what the silly woman

thinks she saw with myself and the

car…

She hesitates outside the front door and whilst I am at the window, I see her stopping in her tracks to open the wage packet. Then she turns around and comes back to ring the bell. I leave watching through the living room window and hurry, faster than I could hurry before my accident, to see what she wants now.

'Now, now, whatever is this?' she is holding the wad of notes in her outstretched hand. 'Just **one** of these will do!' She gives me that grimace of a smile and then adds,' I hope you weren't considering anything underhand… did I tell you my husband Jack is a P.C.V.?'

I swear I can actually feel my blood draining downward. I know my face has turned ashen. I wobble as I stand there in disbelief.

'P.C.V.?' I query, hoping against hope

she has got that wrong.

'Yes, you know... one of those Police

Community Volunteers ...

Also available in paperback by L TAYLOR –some in e book*
(Aka L.A.TAYLOR   LINDA TAYLOR)
From www.amazon.com/author/taylorscribere

1. "DANGEROUS DOLLS" *
2. "MURDER UNMASKED"*
3. "SISTERHOOD" *
4. "TALES OF TWO GINGER TABBY CATS"
5. (Also in large print)
6. "THIRTEEN STRANGE STORIES"
7. "MOLLIE & CO"
8. "MOLLIE ALONE" (The Sequel to MOLLIE & CO)
9. "JACK "
10. "JUST THREE GIRLS"
11. "TELLING DREAMS" *
12. "SECRETS & SORROWS"
13. "OUR BREAD AND BUTTER" (Paperback & Hardback)
14. "MEMORIES & MEMOIRES "
15. "WHO PUT THE DOGS OUT? PLAYERS AT PLAY, FAT" *
16. "THE RESPONSIBLE CHILD" (Paperback & Hardback)
17. "NOT SO PRIVATE LIVES" *
18. *"THE SPECIAL FRIENDSHIP OF SASSY & JIMMY"
19. "IN HER IMAGE" *
20. "ON GOING BACK"*
21. "ONE WEEKEND" *
22. "TO LOVE OR NOT TO LOVE"
23. "NO MORE THROUGH A GLASS DARKLY"
24. "MORE STORIES!"
25. "BEHIND THE SHOP COUNTER"
26. "PAPER CHASE!"   E.T.C.!

Also by L Taylor - in paperback from www.lulupress.com
www.amazon.co.uk www.goodreads.com
"DANGEROUS DOLLS" ... follow up- "MURDER
UNMASKED"
. "TALES OF TWO GINGER TABBY CATS"
" MOLLIE + CO"- follow up- "MOLLIE ALONE" .
"TO GULLS ' REST". "SECRETS & SORROWS".
"13 STRANGE STORIES." followed by
"EXTRAORDINARY STORIES."
"THE MUST READ MEDLEY COLLECTION OF
SHORT STORIES". "SISTERHOOD"."TELLING
DREAMS". "JACK." "JUST THREE GIRLS"." OUR
BREAD AND BUTTER". "WHO PUT THE DOGS OUT,
PLAYERS AT PLAY, FAT." "NOT SO PRIVATE LIVES."

"*I took the doll out of the box and sat her on my dressing table beside
the little bit of make -up I wore; I peered more closely at her face and it
was then I realised what had been told to me; "in her image".
Her painted hair was a reddish brown, long, piled up high in a bun style;
her eyes were also brown but most noticeable of all were her painted red
lips; the lower lip was remarkably fuller than the upper and her ears were
small with little of a lobe... Sitting there, holding her in both hands, she
fascinated me. I thought of her past; who had held her, the circumstances
of their life then... Great Grandmother, Grandmother...I faced my image
in the mirror. There were my brown eyes, my long auburn hair, my
uneven lips and finally, pulling my hair back, those tell-tale ears."*

*So begins Lori's quest to find out more of her ancestors; her mother who
has denied her instincts and her maternal Grandmother and Great
Grandmother and about the "gifts" they had intended her to inherit...
This is a story about the, as yet, unexplained ability some people have to
forsee events before they occur and how Lori must cope with it; described
by some as a gift and also as a curse....*

IN HER IMAGE   AVAILABLE IN PAPERBACK AND E BOOK

NOVELS BY L TAYLOR · AVAILABLE FROM: www.amazon.co.uk www.lulupress.com www.goodreads.com

MOLLIE ALONE
The follow-up of Mollie & Co that sees Mollie coping with widowhood.

TO GULLS' REST
a story about finding love later in life.

13 STRANGE STORIES
Paperback: Thirteen strange stories of supernatural phenomena set in the present that will make you shiver and stop to think about time itself and the very meaning of life and of death...

JACK
A tender story set in the late 1950's, of a young boy's journey from innocence to sexual and emotional awakening, told with humour and nostalgia.

TELLING DREAMS
Someone had told her you cannot die in a dream. They had also said you cannot kill anyone in a dream. But Louisa's recurring dream was like no other. She knew the pain that love could bring...

OUR BREAD AND BUTTER
A part autobiography of the youngest in a family of six children, growing up in a shabby 1960's guest house with competitive siblings, an interfering Victorian paternal grandmother, and "sickly" parents. Seen through the eyes of an innocent and naive nine year old girl.

JUST THREE GIRLS
It is the late 1960's and pop music is rising to a peak of creativity, teenagers have money to spend and jobs to move into whenever they want. Their world is buzzing with pleasure and spending power, which up until now was unheard of for the young. Three teenage girls decide to take a flat together and live the life of the "Swinging Sixties".

THE MUST READ MEDLEY COLLECTION OF SHORT STORIES
A cornucopia of characters and their stories- endearing nostalgic childhood tales (about children and for children) supernatural events, humorous behaviours and vivid character portrayals of coping with love, grief, desire, age...there's something here for everyone!

P.T.O.

CUSTOMER REVIEWS FOR OTHER NOVELS BY L TAYLOR
(https://www.amazon.com/author/ltaylorscribere)

Praise for **"MOLLIE & CO"**
5.0 out of 5 stars
A light hearted tale that makes you smile!
5) By Linda Ferguson on 6 July 2016
I loved this book from the first page.
It is a simple story, an easy read, but I had the hooked from the start. Light-hearted and very funny in places I'm sure there will be many readers who like me, can relate to how Mollie feels at times.
Left me wanting to read more about Mollie and her daily struggles with this new phase in her life.
I hope there will be a sequel!
2) By Ms. T. Lincoln on 26 Jan 2017.
I loved reading this book. Found I couldn't put it down; didn't want it to end

Praise for **"TO GULLS' REST"**
1) By Chrissy on 14 Jan 2015.
Very good read. the author takes you through the ups and downs of complicated and every day

relationships with understanding and compassion but its definitely not sugar coated.
Are one reading this novel will not be at all disappointed its definitely a page turner. Some people may identify with the main character of the book. I think it would definitely transfer well to a film or play. I look forward to the next novel.
2) By S. Thomas on 26 Jan 2015.
This story kept me captivated from start to finish. Very true to how families are, the ups and downs, the love and the differences. I surrounded the in of many families, including my own, and yet it is very individual. This is a great read for holidays, or for a wet weekend. Transporting you into the ordinary and the extraordinary of the everyday life of the heroine. 5.0 out of 5 stars - A great story well told.
2) By Linda Ferguson on 18 December 2014. Verified Purchase.
What a refreshing change! A well written book that meets the reader engaged from start to finish and without the sex or violence so prevalent in today's novels

This could be a story about any family today but it is written with such pathos and understanding it gives a deeper understanding of the emotions that any of us may experience in our lifetime.
Family relationships are often complicated and this family is no exception but somehow as the author introduces each character she has us feeling that we know someone exactly like them, so true is her understanding and description of each personality.
As I read the book I became totally absorbed in what was happening and couldn't wait to see how it would end
Give it a try. You won't be disappointed

View this Author's Spotlight
Gulls' Rest
Paperback, 386 Pages.
by Dee Butler. 31-Mar-2017
Good read, well developed storyline and characters
http://www.lulu.com/spotlight/Goodluckme

Telling Dreams
5 out of 5 stars. Excellent read by Murrey spender on 26 June 2012
Formal Paperback
Excellent read from a new writer. Enjoyed this book very much, had all a good book needs, a good beginning middle and end, or a if the end?

Our Bread And Butter
by Dee Butler. 31-Mar-2017
Enjoyed this story immensely, very sweet from a bygone era.
http://www.lulu.com/spotlight/Goodluckme

PRAISE FOR **"MOLLIE ALONE"**
5.0 out of 5 stars A must read!
18 February 2018.
I've been eagerly awaiting the sequel to Mollie and Co and I must say it was worth the wait! The characters come to life as page after page you feel absorbed feeling what they feel through an the ups and downs and hoping it all works out well in the end. A lovely story with a feel good factor! Thoroughly recommended.

Printed in Great Britain
by Amazon